Tug-of-War

ALL ABOUT BALANCE

Written by Kirsten Hall
Illustrated by Bev Luedecke

children's press®

A Division of Scholastic Inc.
New York Toronto London Auckland Sydney
Mexico City New Delhi Hong Kong
Danbury, Connecticut

About the Author

Kirsten Hall, formerly an early-childhood teacher,
is a children's book editor in New York City. She has been
writing books for children since she was thirteen years old
and now has over sixty titles in print.

About the Illustrator

Bev Luedecke enjoys life and nature in Colorado.
Her sparkling personality and artistic flair are reflected in her
creation of Beastieville, a world filled with lovable Beasties
that are sure to delight children of all ages.

Library of Congress Cataloging-in-Publication Data

Hall, Kirsten.
  Tug-of-war : all about balance / written by Kirsten Hall; illustrated by Bev Luedecke.
    p. cm. — (Beastieville)
  Summary: When the bigger Beasties take on the smaller Beasties in a game of tug-of-war,
they soon learn that size matters.
  ISBN 0-516-22899-4 (lib. bdg.)   0-516-25523-1 (pbk.)
  [1. Tug of war (Game)—Fiction. 2. Size—Fiction. 3. Fairness—Fiction. 4. Stories in rhyme.]
I. Luedecke, Bev, ill. II. Title.
  PZ8.3.H146Tug 2004
  [E]—dc22
                              2004000129

1 2 3 4 5 6 7 8 9 10 R 13 12 11 10 09 08 07 06 05 04

A NOTE TO PARENTS AND TEACHERS

Welcome to the world of the Beasties, where learning is FUN. In each of the charming stories in this series, the Beasties deal with character traits that every child can identify with. Each story reinforces appropriate concept skills for kindergartners and first graders, while simultaneously encouraging problem-solving skills. Following are just a few of the ways that you can help children get the most from this delightful series.

Stories to be read and enjoyed

Encourage children to read the stories aloud. The rhyming verses make them fun to read. Then ask them to think about alternate solutions to some of the problems that the Beasties have faced or to imagine alternative endings. Invite children to think about what they would have done if they were in the story and to recall similar things that have happened to them.

Activities reinforce the learning experience

The activities at the end of the books offer a way for children to put their new skills to work. They complement the story and are designed to help children develop specific skills and build confidence. Use these activities to reinforce skills. But don't stop there. Encourage children to find ways to build on these skills during the course of the day.

Learning opportunities are everywhere

Use this book as a starting point for talking about how we use reading skills or math or social studies concepts in everyday life. When we search for a phone number in the telephone book and scan names in alphabetical order or check a list, we are using reading skills. When we keep score at a baseball game or divide a class into even-numbered teams, we are using math.

The more you can help children see that the skills they are learning in school really do have a place in everyday life, the more they will think of learning as something that is part of their lives, not as a chore to be borne. Plus you will be sending the important message that learning is fun.

Madeline Boskey Olsen, Ph.D.
Developmental Psychologist

Bee-Bop

Puddles

Slider

Wilbur

Zip & Pip

Flippet

Pooky

Mr. Rigby

Smudge

We're the Beasties

Toggles

Once a year, there is a fair.
All the Beasties like to go.

6

There is lots of food to eat.
Then there is a puppet show.

Wilbur does not like the games.
"I have played these games before!"

Toggles knows a different game.
"I know one called tug-of-war!"

"We will need to make two teams.
We will need some long rope, too."

Pooky has a rope at home.
"I will bring one back to you!"

While she goes, they make two teams.
Great big Smudge is on team one.

Puddles wants to be with Smudge.
"Tug-of-war sure sounds like fun!"

Pooky comes back with a rope.
She tells Slider, "I'm with you!"

Zip and Pip come running up.
"Can we be on your team, too?"

Both the teams are ready now.
Toggles says they can begin.

Smudge calls out, "Good luck, team one!"
Zip calls out, "Team two will win!"

"On your mark, get set, and go!"
Team one watches team two fall.

Zip is sad. He stands back up.
"We did not do well at all."

Team two wants another chance.
"This time, we will really try!"

Team two hits the ground again.
Zip and Pip both wonder why.

Smudge is glad they won again.
Bee-Bop shouts, "Hip, hip, hooray!"

Then he starts to do a dance.
Puddles gives a winning spray.

Team two grabs the rope again.
Then they ask for one last try.

Mr. Rigby stops to watch.
"This will not work and I know why!"

"Team one is so very big!
Team two looks so small out there!"

Mr. Rigby wants to help.
He will make teams that are fair.

Smudge is pulling very hard.
Toggles watches everyone.

She says, "Now the teams are fair!
Now the game will be more fun!"

PLAYER COUNT

1. How many of the Beasties are on team one in the beginning?

2. How many of the Beasties are on team one in the end?

3. How many of the Beasties are playing all together?

SOUNDS LIKE...

"Slug" is a word that sounds like "tug." Can you think of any other words that sound like "tug"?

LET'S TALK ABOUT IT

Mr. Rigby wants to make sure that
the game is fair.

1. Why is it important for games to be fair?

2. Have you ever played in a game
that was not fair?

3. Is it more or less fun when two
teams are equal?

WORD LIST

a	everyone	know	rope	time
again	fair	knows	running	to
all	fall	last	sad	Toggles
and	food	like	says	too
another	for	long	set	tug-of-war
are	fun	looks	she	try
ask	game	lots	shouts	two
at	games	luck	show	up
back	get	make	Slider	very
be	gives	mark	small	wants
Beasties	glad	more	Smudge	watch
Bee-Bop	go	Mr.	so	watches
before	goes	need	some	we
begin	good	not	sounds	well
big	grabs	now	spray	while
bring	great	of	stands	why
both	ground	on	starts	Wilbur
called	hard	once	stops	will
calls	has	one	sure	win
can	have	out	team	winning
chance	he	Pip	teams	with
come	help	played	tells	won
comes	hip	Pooky	that	wonder
dance	hits	Puddles	the	work
did	home	pulling	then	year
different	hooray	puppet	there	you
do	I	ready	these	your
does	I'm	really	they	Zip
eat	is	Rigby	this	